MEET THE GIRL TALK CHARACTERS

Sabrina Wells is petite, with curly auburn hair, sparkling hazel eyes, and a bubbly personality. Sabrina loves magazines, shopping, sleepovers, and most of all, she loves talking to her best friends.

Katie Campbell is a straight-A student and super athlete. With her blond hair, blue eyes, and matching clothes, she's everyone's idea of Little Miss Perfect. But Katie has a few surprises for everyone, including herself!

Randy Zak has just moved to Acorn Falls from New York City, and is she ever cool! With her radical spiked haircut and her hip New York clothes, Randy teaches everyone just how much fun it is to be different.

Allison Cloud is a Native American Indian. Allison's supersmart and really beautiful. But she has one major problem: She's thirteen years old, five foot seven, and still growing!

ALLISON TO THE RESCUE!

By L. E. Blair

GIRL TALK® series created by Western Publishing Company, Inc.

Western Publishing Company, Inc., Racine, Wisconsin 53404

Text by B.B. Calhoun

Chapter One

"Here, Charlie," said my father. He reached toward my little brother, who was staggering down our front walk with a huge duffel bag in his arms. "Maybe you'd better let me take that."

"No!" said Charlie, clutching the bag tightly to his chest. "Mary said *I* could carry her bag!"

Mary Birdsong is the college student who lives with my family and helps take care of Charlie and my little sister, Barrett. She's a Native American Chippewa Indian, like everyone in my family. In fact, before she moved in with us, Mary lived on the Chippewa Reservation where my father grew up.

"Okay, Charlie, great job," said Mary as she came down the walk behind him. "Now let's see if your dad's as strong as you are. What do you think? Can he lift it into the trunk by himself?"

Charlie dropped the bag and grinned.

"Bet you can't, Dad," he said, folding his arms

over his chest.

"Nice going, Mary," I whispered to her. Charlie can be kind of difficult sometimes, but Mary definitely has the magic touch when it comes to getting him to cooperate.

She shrugged.

"You know, Allison," she said, "I'm really going to miss Charlie these next two weeks. As a matter of fact, I'm going to miss your whole family."

"I know," I said. "We're definitely going to miss you a lot around here, too." Mary was off to Chicago for a special college study trip.

Just then my mother came out of the house with my baby sister in her arms.

"We came to say good-bye," she said, adjusting Barrett on her hip. "By the way, Mary, did you take the food that Nooma packed up for you?"

Nooma is the Chippewa name my family calls my grandmother. Both of my grandparents live with us, in an addition at the back of our house.

"I sure did," said Mary, holding up a full shopping bag and grinning.

"You'll probably be able to feed everyone on the plane with what she gave you," I joked, thinking of the huge lunches my grandmother packs for me to take to school every day."

Mary laughed.

"I tried to explain to her that they would be serving us a meal on the plane," she said. "But she seemed to think I wasn't going to survive the trip unless I had some home-cooked food with me."

"Come on, Mary," my father called from the driver's seat of the car. "We'd better get moving or we'll be late for your flight."

"Okay, Mr. Cloud," Mary called. The two of us walked toward the car, with Charlie close behind.

"Hey, Mary, I have a good idea," Charlie said suddenly, smiling up at her. "Maybe I could go with you to Chicagoat!"

"It's 'Chicago,' Charlie, not 'Chicagoat,'" I said, laughing. "Don't you think you'd better stay here with us? Mom and Dad would really miss you if you went away."

Charlie's face fell.

"I guess so," he mumbled.

"Listen, Charlie," said Mary, squatting down to look him in the face, "Allison's right. You'd better stay home with your family. I'll be back sooner than you think. Besides, you've got to stay here and take care of Clyde."

Charlie grinned.

"Oh, right!" he said happily. "Hey, it's probably almost time to feed Clyde right now."

I looked at Mary.

"Clyde?" I asked, raising my eyebrows.

"Charlie's imaginary dog," she whispered as she opened the car door and slid in next to my father. "He lives in the invisible doghouse in the backyard."

I held back a giggle.

"Okay, Charlie," I said, tossing my long black ponytail over my shoulder. "Say good-bye to Mary, and then we'll go find out if Clyde is hungry."

We waved as the car drove away, and Charlie took my hand.

"Come on, Allie," he said, pulling me around the house toward the backyard, "I'll show you where Clyde lives."

Clyde's imaginary doghouse turned out to be right under the big chestnut tree that has Charlie's tree house in it.

"What does Clyde like to eat?" I asked.

"He's kind of picky," Charlie explained. "We have to find his special food." He looked around the yard for a moment. "Oh, here's one!" he called. He picked up an acorn and stuck it in the pocket of his jeans.

I was kind of relieved to hear that Clyde liked acorns, because they're pretty easy to find in our backyard. In addition to the big chestnut tree, we have two big oaks, which drop acorns all over the place. I read somewhere that there used to be more oak trees in this area than anywhere else in Minnesota. That's how our town got its name, Acorn Falls. As more people settled here, though, a lot of the trees were cut down to make room for houses.

There are still a lot of trees around my neighborhood, but in some of the newer areas of Acorn Falls the houses are so close together that there are hardly any trees at all. Somehow, it just doesn't make sense to me to cut down trees like that. I mean, I just can't imagine why people would want to live in a place without trees — especially when you think about the fact that trees make oxygen, and people need oxygen to live.

After about ten minutes Charlie's and my pockets were bulging with acorns.

"I think this is probably enough, don't you,

Charlie?" I asked. "We don't want to feed Clyde too many."

"Okay," he said, grabbing a few last acorns. "Now we just have to leave them here for Clyde to find." He bent down and put his acorns on the ground near the base of the chestnut tree.

"Here you go, Clyde. Have a good dinner," I said, adding my acorns to the pile.

"Hey, Allie, you know what?" said Charlie, looking up at me. "Clyde really does eat all his food."

"Well, I guess he's hungry," I said. I stood up and wiped off my hands on my jeans.

"No, really," Charlie insisted. He lowered his voice. "I mean, I know Clyde isn't really, really real, like a real dog," he whispered. "But when Mary and I feed him, by the next day the acorns are gone!"

It was possible that squirrels took the acorns, but I decided that it was probably Mary.

"That is strange, Charlie," I said, making a mental note to remember to come back out to the yard that night after Charlie had gone to bed and get rid of the acorns. "Come on. Let's go inside and see if we can find something for us to eat. I'm starved."

As we walked toward the house, Charlie tugged on the sleeve of my dark blue wool baseball jacket.

"Hey, Allie," he said, looking up at me, "do you think Mom and Dad might let me get a real dog?"

I sighed. Charlie's been asking for a dog practically since he learned to talk. I knew that must be why Mary had helped him invent Clyde.

"I don't know, Charlie," I said, pulling open the back door to our house. "I think Mom and Dad want you to wait until you're a little older."

"Well, I am older now," he said, following me inside. "Maybe they'll change their minds."

I doubted it, since the last time Charlie had asked was only a week before. But I didn't say anything.

When we got inside, we found my mother in the kitchen feeding my baby sister. Barrett was propped up in her infant seat, and my mother was trying to feed her a bottle. Barrett definitely isn't too crazy about formula. Every time my mother got the bottle near her mouth, she shut it tight. I had to admit, I didn't blame her — the yellowish stuff in the bottle didn't look very good to me, either.

"Hi, Mom," I said, reaching for the cookie jar on the counter.

Just then Barrett let out a loud yell, throwing her arms out angrily and knocking her bottle to the floor. When the bottle hit the floor, the top flew off and formula poured out of the bottle.

"Oh, Barrett!" cried my mother.

"Just look at this mess!" she said as she bent down to pick up the bottle.

"Do you want me to help you, Mom?" I asked.

"No, no, that's okay," she said, bending over to wipe up the mess. "I've got it."

Charlie picked that moment to speak up. "Mom, can I get a dog? Please?"

My mother looked up from where she was squatting on the floor and sighed.

"Charlie Cloud, we have discussed this before, and you know the answer," she said.

"But, Mom —" pleaded Charlie.

Just then Barrett began to cry.

"Look, Charlie, this is not the time," said my mother, sounding annoyed.

"Come on, Charlie," I said quickly. "Let's get some cookies and milk and take them to my room. We can sit on my swing together," I added, leading him out of the kitchen.

My swing is one of the things I really love about my room. It's really a swing chair. It's made out of white wicker and has a purple flowered cushion. The swing is outside on my own private terrace, which is another really great thing about my room.

Actually, my whole room is pretty neat. My parents had it built for me when my baby sister, Barrett, was born. Barrett has my old room down the hall. And my three best friends, Randy Zak, Sabrina Wells, and Katie Campbell, helped me pick out the colors for the walls and the bedspread and curtains and stuff. Randy, Sabrina, Katie, and I are all in the seventh grade together at Bradley Junior High.

My room's decorated all in different shades of purple, blue, and gray. Randy, Sabs, Katie, and I got the idea from this magazine article in *Young Chic* about decorating your room to go with your personality type. According to the article, my personality type is "Twilight." I'm not exactly sure what that means, but it is true that I love that time of night right after the sun sets, when everything kind of glows. And I also love the twilight colors we picked for my room.

I led Charlie up the stairs and down the hall to my room. As we opened my french door and stepped out onto my terrace, I saw that his eyes were brimming with tears.

"Hey, Charlie, try not to take it so hard," I said, making room for him next to me on the swing seat. "Mom and Dad just don't want you to take on more than you can handle. Having a pet is a lot of work, you know? They just want you to wait until they're sure you're old enough to be responsible for a dog."

"But I am 'sponsible," he said, his lower lip trembling. "Besides, I've been practicing — with Clyde. I always remember to walk him and feed him. I never, ever forget — just ask Mary."

I looked at him. He looked like he was about to burst into tears.

"Oh, Charlie," I said, putting my arm around his shoulders. "I know. You're right, you do take great care of Clyde. And I'm sure you could learn to take care of a real dog, too."

He looked up at me, his eyes shining.

"Really, Allie?" he asked. "Do you really think so?"

"Sure," I said. "Someday, when you finally do get your dog, I'll bet you really will take good care of it. Here, have a cookie."

But he barely noticed the cookie I held out to him.

"You'll help me, won't you, Allie?" he said, looking up at me.

"Help you?" I repeated.

"Somebody has to tell Mom and Dad I'm 'sponsible," he said. "They'll believe you. I just know it. After all, you're my big sister, right?"

I looked down at his hopeful little face and realized that he probably thought I could do anything — even convince my parents to let him get a dog. I was starting to feel like being Charlie's big sister made me 'sponsible for a few things, too.

Chapter Two

"Hey, Allie, nice threads," said Randy as the two of us walked into the cafeteria the next day at lunch.

I looked down at my oversized black-and-white-striped T-shirt, cropped black leggings, black-and-white-striped socks, and clunky black shoes.

"Thanks," I said.

I had to admit my outfit had actually been a bit inspired by Randy herself. Randy's from New York City, and the way she dresses is sometimes a little on the wild side for Acorn Falls. For example, today she had on a pair of bright-purple crushed-velvet leggings with her black lace-up boots, and a black turtleneck under a purple-and-black zebra-striped silk vest. Randy's hair is pretty wild, too. It's jet-black, like mine, but shorter and kind of spiky.

"Come on," I said, looking across the cafeteria, "I see Sabrina and Katie. Let's go sit down."

But just as we began walking across the room, an eighth-grade guy stepped in front of us and tossed a soda can, basketball-style, into the trash can a few feet away.

"Yes!" he said, holding a fist in the air. "Two points!"

"Hey, Michael Jordan, watch where you throw that can," Randy called to him.

I looked at her. That's one of the amazing things about Randy. She'll say anything to anyone. I mean, at Bradley a lot of the eighth graders will hardly even look at the seventh graders. But Randy doesn't care. If she has something to say, she just says it.

"What was that?" the guy asked, glaring at us and folding his arms across his chest.

"Just what I said," she answered, folding her arms the same way. "That can doesn't belong in that garbage."

"It's recyclable," I explained. "It's supposed to go in one of the bins for cans."

"That's right," added Randy. "So if you care about the planet you call home, you might want to think about using those recycling bins from now on."

The recycling bins were the first project of the environmental club I started at Bradley. The club is called S.A.F.E., which stands for Student Action for the Environment. We had been trying to get people to remember to use the bins, but I had never seen one of our members remind someone quite the way Randy was doing now.

"Oh, yeah," agreed the guy, his face softening. "I heard about that. Are you with that club — S.U.R.E. or something?"

"Actually, it's called S.A.F.E.," I volunteered, stepping forward. "I'm Allison Cloud. I founded the club."

"Cool," said the guy, looking right at me. "I'm Alex — Alex Selby. Hey, listen, a few of us were wondering, can eighth graders join, too? I mean, is it open to everyone?"

"Definitely," I said, without even giving it a second thought. No one outside of the seventh grade had ever asked to join S.A.F.E. before, but I knew we could use all the help we could get. In fact, if enough kids at Bradley got involved, maybe we could work on another project besides recycling.

"Our next meeting is a week from today, next Thursday, after school," I told him. "And anybody who wants to come is welcome."

"Great," said Alex. "I'll let my friends know. And hey, sorry about that soda-can thing. I guess I just wasn't thinking."

"No problem," said Randy, giving him the thumbs-up sign. "Just don't let it happen again, okay?"

"Sure thing," he said, heading over to the trash can and fishing around inside for his soda can. "See you guys next Thursday."

"Randy, you are amazing," I said, shaking my head as we walked over to the table where Sabrina and Katie were sitting.

"What?" she asked.

"Just the way you talked to that guy Alex," I said. "I mean, at first I thought he wanted to sock you or something."

"Yeah," Randy said, grinning, "he did look kind of mad at the beginning, didn't he? But you've got to tell it to people straight if you want to get their attention."

"Well, it definitely worked," I said, putting my lunch bag down on the table and sitting down next to Katie, who was wearing a pale-yellow cable-knit sweater that was almost the color of her silky blond hair. "It sounds like we may have a few new S.A.F.E. members at the next meeting."

"New members? That's great, Allison," said Sabrina, who was sitting across the table. "When is the next meeting, anyway?"

"Next Thursday," I told her, unpacking my chicken-salad sandwich on homemade wheat bread. "We're supposed to be meeting to organize the next recycling drive."

"To get people to volunteer and stuff, right?" said Randy, sitting down next to Sabs.

"Well, actually, a lot of people already signed up in advance at our last meeting," I said. "So everything's pretty much taken care of, at least for a while."

"Then what are we going to do at the meeting?" asked Katie, stirring her yogurt.

"I've been thinking about that," I said, taking a sip of my juice. "And I think maybe S.A.F.E.'s ready to take on another project."

"Like what?" asked Sabrina, her hazel eyes sparkling.

"I'm not sure yet," I said. "But there are plenty of important environmental causes. There's cleaning up the air, for example. We could start a campaign to try to get people to drive their cars less often and ride bikes or walk instead."

"That sounds good," said Randy. "You know, in New York, hardly any of the kids I knew had parents who even owned cars. Mostly everybody just took a lot of buses and subways."

Sabrina giggled.

"Can you imagine subways in Acorn Falls?" she said, her auburn curls bouncing.

"Or we could work on conserving energy," I went on. "For example, how many Bradley students and teachers think of turning off the lights in a classroom between classes or at the end of the day?"

"None, I bet," replied Randy.

"That's true," said Katie. "Sometimes after hockey practice, when there's practically no one in the building, I notice that all the lights are still blazing."

Katie is the only girl on the Bradley hockey team. She stays late at school to practice several times a week.

"That's terrible," said Sabrina.

"Or we could try to raise money to save endangered species," I suggested. "For example, did you know that over half of all the types of animals on the planet live in the rainforests, and that almost a hundred acres of the rainforests are being destroyed every minute?"

"That's so sad," said Katie.

"Really," agreed Sabrina. "It doesn't seem fair. I mean, it's not like the animals can speak up for themselves or anything."

"Then maybe it's up to us to speak for them," I said.

"Sounds good to me, Allie," said Randy.

"Well, then, maybe I'll bring it up at the meeting," I said.

"I'm sure it'll go over well," said Katie. "I mean, everybody likes animals, right?"

"Really," said Sabs. "Who can resist a furry face?"

"Right —" I began. But suddenly I stopped. All this talk about animals was making me think of Charlie and how sad he had looked the day before.

"What is it, Allie?" asked Randy. "Is something wrong?"

"No, no," I said. "I mean, not really. It's just something that happened with Charlie yesterday. You see, he's been asking my parents for a dog. But they won't let him have one."

"Oh, I remember what that was like," said Katie, sighing. "Before I got my cat, Pepper, when

I was little, I asked my mother for months to let me have a kitten. That year when my sister, Emily, and I were making out our Christmas lists, I just wrote *kitten* all over mine."

"I guess that got the point across," I joked.

"I suppose it worked," admitted Katie. "I was so happy when I woke up Christmas morning and saw her under the tree. She was sitting in a little basket with a red ribbon around her neck."

"Aaaww," said Sabrina. "That's so cute."

"She was really little," Katie said, thinking. "But then it was amazing how fast she grew. Now she's such a part of me that I can't imagine my life without her."

"I know," said Sabrina. "Cinnamon is like a member of our family. We've had her since I was five."

Cinnamon is the Wells family's dog. Sabs says she's half German shepherd and half golden retriever. She's very big and very friendly.

"I always kind of thought it would be cool to have a pet," said Randy. "But they weren't allowed in the apartment building where we lived in New York. I mean, goldfish and hamsters and stuff were okay, but we couldn't have anything big like a dog or a cat."

"Dogs are great," said Sabs. "When I get home from school, Cin is always there to meet me at the door. And she can really tell when I'm feeling bad. She even licks the tears off my cheeks when I cry."

"So what's the deal, Allison?" asked Randy. "If dogs are so great, why won't your parents let Charlie have one?"

"I think they're worried that he might not be ready to take care of a pet," I said. "They say they want him to wait until he's a little older."

"A pet can be a lot of work," said Katie. "But I think having Pepper made me more responsible. I mean, for the first time in my life, I had to take care of someone."

"That's a good point, Katie," I said. "After all, how's Charlie supposed to learn to be responsible if he doesn't have anything to be responsible for?"

"Really," said Randy. "Your parents ought to be able to understand that."

"Yeah," I said. I thought a moment. "I guess it's going to be up to me to explain it to them."

"Oh, I'm sure they'll listen to you," said Sabrina. "They always listen to the oldest."

"Sabs is right," agreed Katie. "Sometimes I

feel I could try to explain something to my mother forever, but if Emily just mentions it once, then suddenly she pays attention."

"Sounds pretty frustrating to me," said Randy.

Randy doesn't have any brothers or sisters. Her parents are divorced, and she lives alone with her mother.

"Oh, but sometimes it can work out really well, too," said Katie quickly. "Like the time when I was younger and my grandparents were having this big, fancy anniversary party. Emily was the one who convinced my mother that I was old enough to pick out my own dress for it."

"I guess you're right, Katie," said Sabs. "My older brothers are always saying that Sam and I are the lucky ones, because they've already 'broken in' my parents for us."

In addition to her twin brother, Sam, Sabrina has three older brothers. Actually, even Sam is older than Sabs — by four minutes, a fact he never lets her forget.

"I guess you guys are right," I said. "Charlie could really use my help with this one."

"Hey, that's what older sisters are for, right?" said Randy. "I mean, even I know that."

I nodded. My mind was made up. I decided

to talk to my parents as soon as possible about letting Charlie get a dog.

Chapter Three

I waited to talk to my parents until dinner that night, when I knew the whole family would be together.

By the time I sat down at the table, my mother and father were at their places at either end of the table, and my grandparents were sitting in their usual spots across from me. Barrett was in her infant seat near my mother. But Charlie was missing.

"Do you know where Charlie is?" my father asked.

"I called him five minutes ago," my mother said, starting to serve the salad. "He said something about doing something important, but he promised to be here in a minute."

"I can't imagine what that boy thinks is more important than dinner," said my grandmother, sliding a square of lasagna onto a plate and setting it on the table in front of Charlie's empty chair.

I had to admit, I couldn't imagine anything more important to Charlie than his dinner. It wasn't like him to be late.

Suddenly I had an idea.

"I think I know where he is," I said, standing up and pushing back my chair.

"Allison, where are you going?" asked my mother.

"I'll be right back," I said. I hurried out of the dining room and through the kitchen to the back door.

There was only one thing I could think of that might be more important to Charlie than his own dinner — Clyde's dinner. Sure enough, I found him crouched in the backyard under the chestnut tree with a pile of acorns on the ground in front of him.

"Come on, Charlie," I said, putting my hand on his shoulder. "Everybody's waiting inside."

"I had to feed Clyde," he said, looking up at me.

"Okay," I said, "I know. But now you'd better get in and feed yourself, before your dinner gets cold."

I looked at him.

"Besides," I said, grinning, "I need you in

there with me when I talk to Mom and Dad about why they should let you get a dog."

His face lit up.

"Are you really going to, Allie?" he asked excitedly, jumping up. "Do you really mean it? You're going to tell them I'm 'sponsible?"

"Sure," I said, laughing and giving him a little hug. "Or at least, I'm going to tell them I think you can learn to be 'sponsible. Let me do most of the talking. Don't you say anything about it until I say it's time, okay?"

"Okay, Allie," Charlie answered. He began galloping happily toward the house. "I won't say anything about a dog — not till you tell me it's time."

When we got back inside, everybody had already started eating.

"Well, there they are," said my father, looking up from his lasagna. "I thought we might have to send the dogs out after you two."

Charlie perked up.

"Dogs?" he asked excitedly.

I nudged him under the table with my foot, and he looked at me.

"It's just an expression, Charlie," I whispered.

He nodded.

"Don't worry, Allie," he whispered back. "I won't say anything till you say it's time."

"What's that whispering over on that side of the table?" my grandmother asked as she sprinkled grated cheese on her lasagna.

I knew I was going to have to say something soon, before Charlie spilled the beans. Especially since it was starting to seem like my family would go on talking about dogs all night. But how should I bring it up? Finally I decided that the best way to do it was quickly and honestly.

I took a deep breath.

"Mom, Dad, I'd like to talk to you about something," I began.

Charlie perked up. I knew he could tell what was coming.

"Yes, sweetheart, what is it?" asked my mother.

"Well, it's not exactly anything you haven't heard about before," I said. "But I think I may have some new things to say about it, and I'd really like you to listen to everything I have to say before you answer."

"All right, Allison," said my father. "That sounds fair enough. You have the floor. Go ahead and state your case."

It's not exactly hard to tell by the way he talks that my father is a lawyer. I think he forgets that real life isn't a courtroom. Like he always expects people to be totally logical. Sometimes, though, it's kind of helpful to have certain rules that everyone agrees to follow in a conversation, like they do in court. I hoped this was going to be one of those times.

"Well," I said, taking a deep breath, "what I'd like to say is that I think there might be some very good reasons that you haven't thought of in considering whether Charlie can get a puppy."

I must have been kind of nervous, because the last part of the sentence all came out at once, in a rush. I think it took a moment for what I was saying to sink in with my parents, but as soon as it did, they both began talking.

"Oh, Allison," my mother began, "I know you mean well —"

"Your mother and I have already discussed this," my father was saying, "and our answer is no —"

"Mom, Dad, hold on a minute," I said, a little frustrated. "You told me I could finish what I had to say."

My father looked at me.

"You're right," he said. "That was our agreement. Go ahead."

I looked at Charlie, who was sitting so close to the edge of his seat that it looked like he might fall off. His eyes were glued on me. I thought about what Randy had said, about this being what older sisters were for, and I sat up straighter in my chair.

"I know you're worried about whether or not Charlie can handle taking care of a dog," I said, looking from my mother to my father. "But having a pet might actually help Charlie learn to be responsible. I mean, think of it this way — if Charlie had a dog, he would have to learn to take care of someone."

"Now, I know that may sound like a good idea, Allison," said my father, "but I'm just not sure Charlie's ready for that kind of responsibility."

"Maybe when he gets a little older," said my mother.

I glanced at Charlie, who looked like he was blinking back tears. I didn't know what else to say. I had tried, but it just wasn't working.

Suddenly my grandfather spoke up.

"You know" — he wiped his mouth with his

napkin — "a dog can be a boy's best friend." He looked at my father. "Why, I remember that old mutt you had when you were a kid. That dog followed you just about everywhere. What was his name?"

"Tiger," said Nooma. "He was a stray — just showed up one day at the house and wouldn't leave."

I stared at my father. This was something I had never heard about.

"You had a dog, Dad?" I asked.

"Well, yes, I did," my father answered. "But that was completely different."

I looked at Charlie, who looked back at me, his eyes shining.

"Why was it so different?" I asked.

"Well, first of all, I was a lot older than Charlie is," said my father.

"How old were you, Nathan?" asked my mother.

"Oh, well, I don't know," my father sputtered. "I must have been at least —"

"Eight," said Nooma.

Suddenly Charlie couldn't hold it in any longer.

"Hey, I'm seven and a quarter!" he said, sitting up very tall.

"Well, I'm sure I must have been older than that, Nooma," said my father.

"No, I distinctly remember," said my grandmother. "I was in the kitchen, baking a cake for your eighth birthday, when the dog showed up at the back door. I gave you a bowl of scraps to feed him, and from then on, he was your dog."

She speared a cucumber in her salad bowl and lifted her fork to her mouth.

"In fact," she added, looking at my father, "it was the day before your eighth birthday, so I suppose you could say you were really still only seven."

"Dad! Dad!" Charlie was yelling. "I'm seven, too! Can't I get a dog like you did?"

All the commotion must have gotten Barrett excited, because she started making lots of noises and waving her arms around in her seat.

"Now, hold on just a minute," my father said, looking around the table at all of us. "All right, so maybe I was Charlie's age when I had Tiger. But I still say things were completely different."

"How so?" asked my mother gently.

"Well, for one thing, I was a very mature eight-year-old," said my father. "I was very independent. Isn't that right, Nooma?"

"Sure," said Nooma, chewing, "you went all over the reservation by yourself."

"There," said my father, looking around at us triumphantly. "You see?"

"I used to worry myself sick," Nooma went on. "You were always getting into some kind of trouble — throwing water balloons or drawing with chalk on the side of the schoolhouse. And then there was that time you took the neighbor girl's cap and threw it in the middle of the frozen pond. Poor Grandpa had to go out there and get it."

I stared at my father, amazed. This was definitely a side of him I had never heard about.

"It was a good thing that dog came along when it did," Nooma was saying. "Kept you out of trouble. I guess you were just bored before that. You just needed a friend to keep you busy."

"Nathan," my mother said to my father, "it sounds to me like maybe having a dog was a positive influence on you."

"I suppose it was," said my father. "He was a good dog, too. He had these funny dark marks on his back, like stripes. That was why I named him Tiger."

I cleared my throat.

"Dad," I said, "there's another thing I'd like to say. You didn't have an older sister to help you learn how to be responsible for your dog. If you let Charlie get one, I promise I'll teach him how to take care of it."

My parents looked at each other and smiled.

"It's all right with me if it's all right with you," my mother said to my father.

"Well, then, it's all right with me, too," said my father, smiling. "Charlie, you can have your dog."

Before I could say a word, Charlie leaped out of his chair and threw his arms around my neck.

"Oh, Allie," he said happily, "you're the best big sister in the whole wide world."

I hugged him back as hard as I could. Just hearing him say that made the whole dog discussion worthwhile.

Chapter Four

"Allie! Allie!" Charlie was yelling. "Come on, let's go!"

I opened my eyes and stretched. Suddenly I remembered — it was Saturday, the day Charlie and I were supposed to go to the Acorn Falls Animal Shelter to pick out his dog. Nooma was going, too, because a grown-up had to be there when you got your dog.

"Allie, come on!" Charlie yelled again from outside my door.

"Okay, Charlie!" I called back. "Just give me a minute to get ready. Go eat your breakfast and I'll meet you downstairs."

I could hear his footsteps disappear as he ran down the hall away from my room. I sat up in bed and looked around. I love the way my room looks in the morning. There's a long line of windows that runs along three of my walls, and I can see the trees in our backyard through them. In the morning the sunlight makes the leaves glow.

I got out of bed and pulled on a dark blue sweater and my favorite pair of jeans. Then I put on a pair of tan boots and brushed my hair. I checked myself quickly in my full-length mirror, and grabbed my jacket before heading downstairs.

When I walked into the kitchen, my grandmother was at the sink, washing dishes. Charlie was at the table, just finishing his bowl of cereal.

"Hi, Allie!" said Charlie, jumping up from his chair as soon as he saw me. "I'm ready. Can we go now?"

My grandmother sighed.

"Just wait a moment and let your sister get some breakfast first," she told him. She turned to me. "That boy's been bouncing around this house like a jumping bean since early this morning. He must have been up and down those stairs to your room thirty times."

"He's excited," I said, opening the refrigerator. "I'll just grab something quick so we can get started right away." I pulled out the loaf of banana-walnut bread my grandmother had baked the day before and cut a thick slice.

My grandmother scowled.

"Is that all you're having?" she asked me. "Come, let me make you some oatmeal, too."

"That's okay, Nooma. This is fine," I said, holding the slice in one hand and grabbing Charlie with the other. "I can eat something else when we get back if I'm still hungry."

Nooma saw she didn't have a chance, so she just got her coat and joined us at the door. Nooma's always had this thing about feeding people. If she had her way, I'd probably always be eating four-course meals for breakfast, lunch, and dinner.

Out in front of our house, I helped Charlie zip his jacket and took his hand. Nooma walked behind us. The Acorn Falls Animal Shelter is on Dillard Street, which is about a fifteen-minute walk from our house, on the outskirts of town. I had never actually been there before, but I knew that was where all the stray animals in Acorn Falls were taken. It made me feel good to know that we would be adopting an animal that really needed a home.

As Charlie, Nooma, and I rounded the corner onto Green Street, we almost bumped right into Billy Dixon. Billy's in my class at school, and he's one of my really good friends. He lives on

Callahan Drive, which is not too far from Green Street.

"Hey, Allie!" Billy said, surprised. "What are you doing around here?" He looked down at my brother. "And my man Charlie! How're you doing?" Then he nodded at Nooma. "Mrs. Cloud," he added.

Billy tugged up the sleeve of his black leather bomber jacket, bent down, and put out his hand for Charlie, who grinned and smacked the open palm as hard as he could. I winced, thinking it must have hurt, but Billy didn't even seem to notice.

"Hi, Billy," I said, smiling at him.

"Guess what, Billy?" Charlie broke in excitedly. "I'm going to get a puppy!"

"A puppy, huh?" said Billy, looking at me. I nodded. "Wow, Charlie, that's great."

"Allie and Nooma and me are going to pick him out right now," Charlie told him. "At the Animal Seller."

"That's the Animal Shelter, Charlie," I said, laughing.

"Sounds like fun," said Billy, grinning and shaking a lock of his brown hair off his forehead.

"Hey, why don't you come with us?" I asked.

"Yeah, Billy!" said Charlie, hopping up and down. "Come with us!"

Billy hesitated.

"Are you sure?" he asked. "I mean, I don't want to butt in on a family-type thing, or anything."

"It's all right with you, Nooma, isn't it?" I asked.

She nodded and smiled.

"Sure, come on," I said. "It'll be fun. You can help us pick out the dog."

"Okay," said Billy, grinning, his blue eyes sparkling.

We took off down Green Street, with Charlie between us and Nooma walking behind us.

"Dogs are great," Billy said. "We used to have one when I was little. It was a poodle."

"A *poodle*?" I said and burst out laughing. Somehow, the idea of tough Billy Dixon with a fluffy little poodle was really funny. I would have expected him to have something bigger and more rugged, like a German shepherd or a Doberman.

"Actually, it was my mom's dog," Billy explained. "She named it Bijou, which means 'jewel' in French. She taught it tricks, too — like if you held a dog biscuit right above its nose, it would walk around on its hind legs and stuff." He shook his head. "My mom used to spoil it, though — give it food from the table and stuff. It made my father so mad."

I looked at Billy. He had kind of a faraway look in his eyes. I didn't know what to say. Billy's mother died when he was pretty little, and I knew he must miss her.

But before I could say anything, he snapped out of it.

"So, Charlie," he said, grinning down at my brother. "What do you think you're going to name this dog of yours?"

"That's easy," said Charlie. "Clyde Junior."

Billy laughed.

"An interesting choice," he said.

"Oh, Charlie," I said, "are you sure? I mean, isn't Clyde Junior kind of a long name for a dog?"

"I can just hear you guys out in your backyard now," said Billy, still laughing. "'Clyde Junior! Oh, Clyde Junior! Here, Clyde Junior!'"

"Charlie, maybe you want to wait till you pick out your dog before you pick out a name," I suggested. "That way you can be sure to choose something that's just right."

"Well," said Charlie. "I guess you're right."

"Looks like you're about to get your chance, Charlie," remarked Billy as we turned the corner onto Dillard Street. "I think that's it up ahead."

I looked up the street and saw a red-brick one-story building with a small sign in front that read ACORN FALLS ANIMAL SHELTER. I had to admit, I was a little surprised at how small and plain the shelter looked. Not that I had been expecting anything fancy. But there weren't even any windows. And the ground around the building was just dry, brown dirt, with no grass or trees or anything. Next door was a big empty lot filled with garbage and broken glass.

We walked up to the building and climbed the cement steps to the door. I pulled it open, jingling the bells hanging on the back, and we stepped into a small waiting room. On one side of the room was a wobbly-looking desk and two metal folding chairs. Across from that was a worn-out brown corduroy couch. The whole place looked kind of dingy and dark, except for the walls, which were covered with tons of pictures of animals — from cats and dogs to rabbits and zebras — that looked like they had been cut out of magazines and stuck up with tape.

Just then a door opened on the other side of

the room, and I could hear lots of barking and yapping. A short older woman walked in, closing the door behind her. She wore her gray hair in a bun that had loose strands escaping from it on all sides.

"Oh, hello, there," she said, smiling at the four of us. "I thought I heard the bell. I'm Miss Peabody, and I run the shelter. How can I help you today?"

"I'm getting a puppy." Charlie beamed.

"We'd like to adopt a dog," I explained.

"Oh, well, isn't that lovely," Miss Peabody said. "I'm always so happy to find a good home for one of my animals. You'll have to wait a few minutes, though, while I go back and get things set up for you. Have a seat on the couch, please."

I looked at Billy as Miss Peabody disappeared back behind the door.

"What do you think she meant by that?" I asked. "I mean, what kind of setting up would she have to do?"

Billy shrugged.

"Beats me," he said.

"It seems a little strange," I said, thinking. "You'd think she'd just take us back right away and just let us see the animals."

"Look! Look!" Charlie called out suddenly laughing. "Come see this funny picture."

We walked over to where he was standing, pointing to one of the magazine pictures taped to the wall. The picture was of this really tall, skinny dog with incredibly long, straight, white fur and a pointy black snout. The caption said AFGHAN.

"Hey, Charlie, are you getting a dog like that?" joked Billy.

Charlie laughed.

"I hope not," I said. "I'd hate to think of how long it would take to give it a shampoo."

"Yeah, you'd probably have to send it to a barber or a beauty parlor or something," said Billy, grinning.

Just then Miss Peabody opened the door again.

"All right," she said, smiling. "We're all ready for you. Just follow me, please."

"Yippee!" said Charlie happily. "Come on, guys, it's time to get my dog!"

We followed her through the door and down a hallway, with Charlie skipping along excitedly. There were several doors on either side of the hall, but she led us straight to the first one on the right, which had a hand-lettered sign that said VISITORS' ROOM taped to it.

"Here we are," she announced cheerfully, pushing open the door. "Now you just take your time and look around. I'm sorry, but I won't be able to stay with you. There are a few other things to take care of, and I'm rather short-staffed here. But I'll be back in a few minutes, and you can tell me what you've decided."

She hurried away down the hall, and Nooma, Billy, and I followed Charlie into the room.

As soon as we stepped inside, the barking began. There were quite a few cages in the room — and inside each cage was a puppy. Suddenly it seemed like every puppy there was barking at us.

"Wow," said Charlie, looking around, his eyes wide.

"Just look at all these dogs!" said Billy.

Suddenly I felt a pang of sadness. Obviously, every one of these dogs deserved a good home. It made me feel kind of bad to think that we could only take one of them. Well, I thought, maybe the others would get adopted soon, too.

I looked around at the cages. Every type of dog seemed to be there — big, little, short-haired, long-haired, floppy-eared, spotted — you name it. I wondered how we would ever be able to choose.

But suddenly Charlie was calling out to me.

"Look! Look!" he said, hurrying over to a cage in the corner. "I think this one likes us!"

I walked over to the cage and looked at the puppy inside. He was light tan, with beautiful shiny, shaggy hair. He was standing on his hind legs, looking right at us and wagging his tail. Charlie put his fingers up to the cage, and the puppy pushed his wet black nose through the bars to lick Charlie's hand.

"Ooooh!" Charlie giggled. "That tickles."

I bent down and put my fingers through the bars and stroked the soft tan fur of the puppy's head.

"Aw," Nooma said. "He's a sweetie."

"That's one nice-looking dog," said Billy, squatting down beside me to look in the cage.

The dog looked back at Billy and barked.

We all laughed.

"See?" said Charlie. "He wants us to take him home!" He looked back to me. "He wants to be my dog."

"Well, Allie?" said Billy, looking at me. "What do you say? That sounds like a decision to me."

"Charlie, are you sure this is the dog you want?" I asked.

"I'm sure he's the one," said Charlie, gazing into the cage, "and he's sure I'm the one, too."

The puppy let out a long whine and wagged his tail.

"All right," Nooma said, laughing. "He's the one."

"I'll go find Miss Peabody and tell her we've made up our minds," offered Billy.

"Thanks, Billy," I said. "I'm sure she's around here somewhere."

I turned to Charlie.

"Well," I asked, "now that you've seen him, what do you think you want to name him?"

Charlie thought a moment.

"I don't know," he said. He turned to the puppy. "What's your name, doggie?" he asked.

The puppy looked right back at him and barked once — *"Ruff!"*

Charlie stared, wide-eyed.

"Ralph!" he said happily. "Did you hear that, Allie? Nooma? He said his name is Ralph!"

"Sounds good to me, Charlie," I said, laughing. I had to admit I was just happy he had given up the "Clyde Junior" idea.

Just then Miss Peabody came into the room.

"Well?" she asked, smiling. "How's it going in here? Have you made a choice yet?"

"Well, yes, we have," I said, looking around for Billy. I realized that he was probably still looking through the building. He and Miss Peabody must have missed each other somehow.

"We want this one over here," Charlie said happily, pointing to the cage. "His name is Ralph."

"Well, isn't that a lovely name!" she said, pulling a huge key ring out of the pocket of her dress. "All right, Ralph," she said, bending down to open the cage, "come on out and meet your new owners."

Just then I noticed Billy slip back into the room. He had a funny look on his face, like something was really bothering him. I wondered what it could be.

But suddenly Ralph was out of his cage and all over Charlie, jumping on him and covering his face with kisses.

"Look!" Charlie cried happily. "He likes me!"

"He sure does, Charlie," I said, bending down to stroke the dog's head. "Welcome to the Cloud family, Ralph."

Chapter Five

"Oh, look how cute he is!" cried Sabrina, looking down at the puppy in my brother's arms.

"His name's Ralph," Charlie said proudly.

"He's adorable," cooed Katie, reaching out to stroke Ralph behind the ears.

"I like his coloring. His fur is so shiny. And his big floppy ears are adorable!" said Randy, grinning.

"I know," I said. "Isn't he sweet? You should have seen how many others there were at the shelter. I wanted to take them all home."

It was Saturday evening, and Randy, Katie, and Sabs had come over to my house for a sleepover. Charlie and Nooma and I had been back from the shelter for a few hours, but Charlie had barely let Ralph out of his arms. I had never seen my brother look so happy. His biggest wish had come true.

Just then my parents walked into the living

room, where we were all sitting. My father was wearing a suit, and my mother had on a really pretty blue dress, with her black hair tucked up in a french twist.

"Wow, Mom, you look great," I said.

She smiled.

"Thanks, honey," she said, patting a hair into place. "Your father and I are meeting the Wolfsons for dinner. Right now Nooma's feeding Barrett in the kitchen, but she says to tell you all that your dinner will be on the table in a few minutes."

"Now, we're counting on you to kind of keep an eye on things, Allison," said my father, helping my mother on with her coat. "Especially now with Mary gone and the puppy here."

"Yes," added my mother, "maybe you could try to take Barrett off Nooma's hands a little later."

"Sure, Mom and Dad," I said. "I'll take care of everything."

"And, Charlie, you go to bed when your sister tells you, right?" said my father.

"Okay," said Charlie. I could see that he was still so busy gazing down at Ralph that he had barely heard what my father had said.

"We shouldn't be too late," called my mother, heading toward the door. "Have fun."

A few minutes later my grandmother called us all to dinner. We headed into the dining room and took our places around the table as she put a piece of chicken on each of our plates and started spooning out the mashed potatoes.

"Mmmm," said Sabrina, taking her place, "smells good."

Charlie slid into his chair with Ralph in his arms, and I saw my grandmother scowl.

"There'll be no dogs sitting at this table, young man," she said, pointing her serving spoon at him sternly.

Charlie pouted.

"Oh, please, Nooma?" he begged, clutching Ralph to his chest. "Ralph wants to stay with me."

"Hey, Charlie, it's going to be pretty tough to eat if you're using both arms to hold Ralph," Randy pointed out.

"I know, Charlie," I said. "Let's put Ralph down on the floor, under the table. That way he can wait there till you're done eating."

"Well, all right," he said, reluctantly letting the puppy out of his arms.

"That's more like it," said my grandmother, wiping her hands on her apron. "Now, everything you need is on the table. I'm going back into the kitchen to check on the baby. Your grandfather's watching her, but I think he'd like to get back to our place and relax a little."

"I'll come in and get Barrett when we're done eating, Nooma," I told her. "That way you can go back home with Grandpa."

A little while later, as we were finishing dinner, Katie suddenly looked under the table.

"Hey," she said, "did somebody give Ralph a bone or something?"

"They better not have," said Sabrina, alarmed. "Chicken bones are bad for dogs, especially puppies."

"I didn't give him anything," I said.

"Neither did I," said Charlie.

"Well, then, what's that he's chewing under there?" asked Randy, looking down by her feet.

I pushed back my chair and stuck my head under the table. It was kind of dark down there, but there was no doubt about it, Ralph definitely had something in his mouth, and he was gnawing on it pretty steadily.

"Ralph," I said, crawling under the table.

"Ralph, what do you have?"

As soon as he saw me coming, Ralph backed away.

"Katie, he's over on your side," I called. "See if you can grab him."

Katie's head appeared under the table, but Ralph moved quickly away from her.

"Oh, I can't reach him," she said, stretching her arms out toward him. "Charlie, he's headed toward you!"

Charlie bent down and crawled under the table.

"Don't worry!" he called out. "I got him. Give me that, Ralphie."

There was a short scuffle, a couple of loud barks, and then Charlie poked his head out from under the table.

"I got it! I got it!" he shouted, waving something in his hand.

"What is it, Charlie?" I asked.

He looked at the object in his hand.

"Uh-oh," he said. "It's Dad's slipper."

"Dad's slipper?" I asked, standing up. "How did Ralph get that?"

I walked over to Charlie and took the slipper out of his hand. Ralph peered out at me from under the table.

"Ralph!" I said sternly, bending down to put the slipper in front of his nose. "No! Bad dog!"

"Oh, no, Allie!" Charlie pleaded, throwing his arms around Ralph. "Please don't get mad at him. He won't do it again. He promises."

"Charlie, you have to start teaching Ralph right from wrong while he's still a puppy," I explained. "Otherwise he'll just keep doing stuff like this."

"That's true, Charlie," said Sabrina. "It's important to train him while he's still young."

"You know what they say, Charlie," said Randy. "'You can't teach an old dog new tricks.'"

"I guess so," said Charlie.

"Here," I said, handing him the slipper, "why don't you try it? You don't have to scream at him or anything. Just make sure he understands that what he did was wrong. It's one of the things you have to do to become responsible for Ralph."

Charlie squatted down on the floor next to Ralph with the slipper.

"Ralph," he said, holding the slipper where Ralph could see it, "I guess you really weren't supposed to chew Dad's slipper. I know it was an accident, though, and I know you won't do it again." He patted Ralph on the head. "Good dog."

"Wow, that's telling him," joked Randy.

"Well, I guess it's a start," I said with a sigh. "Go on, Charlie. Take Ralph into the living room while I go get Barrett from Nooma. We'll be in, in a minute."

When we walked into the living room, we found Charlie and Ralph in the middle of the room, playing a kind of tug-of-war. Charlie was holding something in his hand, and Ralph had the other end in his mouth. Every time Charlie pulled, Ralph would growl playfully, and whenever Ralph pulled, Charlie would burst out laughing.

All of a sudden I realized what they were tugging on — one of the little brown flowered pillows from our couch!

"Charlie!" I said quickly. "What are you doing? You're going to rip that pillow!"

Charlie looked up at me in surprise and suddenly let go of the pillow. Ralph was still pulling on the pillow as hard as he could with his mouth. He went flying backward, knocking into the stand where we keep our fireplace tools, which came crashing down around him. The noise must have scared him, because he let out a loud bark and went running across the room, ending up under the couch.

The whole thing got Barrett pretty excited, and she started bouncing up and down in my arms.

"Eeeee! Eeeeee!" she yelled happily.

I didn't know what to do first — get mad at Charlie, quiet Barrett, fish Ralph out from under the couch, or clean up the tools. But just then Randy let out a shriek.

"Eeeew!" she yelled, looking down at the carpet. "I just stepped in a puddle! Who spilled something?"

Sabrina bent down to look at the wet stain on the carpet.

"I've got news for you, Ran," she said. "No one spilled anything. But I do know who did it. The culprit is hiding under the couch."

"Yuck!" said Randy, shaking her foot. "My sock is totally soaked. Ugh, why did I ever take off my shoes?"

"Why don't you go upstairs and borrow a pair of my socks from my dresser, Randy," I said. "Meanwhile I'll start teaching Charlie how to clean up after Ralph."

"Me?" asked Charlie. "Why do I have to do it?"

"Because he's your dog," I told him. "And this is part of what it means to be responsible for him."

"Here, Allie," said Katie, reaching out to me. "I'll hold Barrett for you if you want."

I passed Barrett to Katie and led Charlie into the kitchen. We took a bucket out from under the sink and filled it with soapy water.

"Okay," I said, taking the bucket out to the living room and handing Charlie a sponge. "Start using this. I'm going to take Ralph outside. I think this is his way of telling us that he needs to be walked." I turned to Katie. "You can take Barrett into the den if you want," I told her. "There are a lot of her toys and stuff in there."

But Ralph was no longer under the couch. In fact, I couldn't find him anywhere.

"Oh, no," I cried. "I wonder what he's chewing now."

"I'll help you look for him, Allie," said Sabs.

Ten minutes later we found him in the closet near the front door with his head inside one of my grandfather's gigantic green rubber boots.

"Gotcha!" I cried, pulling him out and picking him up.

"Wow," said Sabrina. "This pooch definitely has a thing for footwear."

I reached for the red leash hanging from the doorknob and hooked it onto his collar.

"Come on, Ralph," I said. "It's time to go outside."

Just then I heard Charlie call me from the living room.

"Allie! Allie!" he cried. "Come quick! I need some help!"

I tucked Ralph under one arm, the leash dangling behind me, and walked back into the living room with Sabrina.

Charlie was on his hands and knees, with the bucket of water on its side nearby, and a huge dark wet spot on the rug in front of him.

"I was trying to be 'sponsible," he said, looking up at me with the sponge in his hand, "but the puddle just keeps getting bigger."

"Oh, no!" I said, letting go of Ralph and hurrying over to Charlie. "I didn't mean for you to pour the bucket of water on the rug, Charlie!"

He looked up at me, his lower lip trembling.

"Watch out!" said Sabrina suddenly. "There goes Ralph!"

Ralph had taken off and was running around

the room, his leash trailing after him like some kind of long red tail.

"Catch him!" I cried, springing to my feet.

"Here, Ralph! Here, Ralphie!" called Charlie, running after him.

Ralph dodged through our legs and flew around the couch. Suddenly his leash got caught on the leg of one of the end tables. The table wobbled, and the plant on top of it began to tip.

"Oh, no!" I yelled. "The plant!"

"I got it! I got it!" called Sabrina, who had run over and stuck out her hand just in time to steady it as Ralph ran out of the room.

"He's in the den!" cried Charlie. "I saw him go in the den!"

"Come on," I said. "We've got him cornered in there. There's no other way out."

We could hear loud barks and growls coming from the den.

"Oh, no!" cried Katie's voice. "Ralph, stop that! Leave that alone!"

I hurried into the den, with Sabrina and Charlie close behind me.

Katie was standing with Barrett in her arms, looking down at Ralph, who was growling and barking at one of the stuffed toys in Barrett's playpen. The toy was a giant stuffed dog, and Ralph kept trying to stick his nose between the bars of the playpen to get to it.

"I don't believe it!" I said, laughing. "He probably thinks it's another dog in a cage, like the ones at the shelter!"

"That's so funny!" said Sabrina, laughing.

But Barrett definitely didn't think it was funny at all. As soon as she heard Ralph barking and growling, she began to cry.

"Oh, Barrett, don't cry, sweetie," said Katie, bouncing her up and down a little.

But Barrett just cried harder, and all that crying was just making Ralph bark more.

Just then Randy walked into the room.

"Phew, that's better!" she said. Then she looked around. "Hey, what's going on in here?" she asked. "Well, for one thing, I'm taking this little monster out for a walk." Randy scooped Ralph up and headed out the door.

"Thanks, Randy," I called after her over Barrett's cries. "Here, Katie," I said, reaching out for my sister. "Maybe you'd better let me take her."

Somehow, in the next half hour, Katie, Sabs, and I managed to quiet Barrett down, clean up the mess in the living room, and tuck Barrett and Charlie into bed. By the time we were done, everyone was exhausted.

"Boy," said Sabrina, as the three of us flopped down on the couch in the living room. "That was really incredible."

"Hey," I said, looking around suddenly, "where's Randy?"

"Shouldn't she and Ralph be back from their walk by now?" said Katie.

The front door suddenly opened, and Randy walked in, with Ralph straggling along behind her.

"There," she said triumphantly. "That ought to take care of the little monster for a while."

"What happened, Randy?" I asked. "We were expecting you a while ago."

"Really," said Sabs. "You've been out there a long time."

Randy grinned.

"I decided to give old Ralph a taste of his own medicine," she said. "So we ran up and down the block a few times — about fifty times."

Sabs laughed.

"He sure looks pooped," she said.

"He'd better be," said Randy, flopping into an

armchair. "I sure am."

Ralph curled up on the floor by my feet and immediately fell sound asleep.

"Thanks, Randy," I said. "Thank you all. I don't know what I would have done without you tonight."

A moment later the front door opened again.

"Hi," called my mother, walking into the house. "We're home."

"Hi, Mom. We're in here," I called.

"Well, just look at this," said my father, peering in the doorway of the den and looking around at the four of us and the sleeping dog. "It seems like you girls had a pretty quiet evening."

"Oh, good," said my mother, peeking in after him. "I'm glad everything went smoothly."

"That Ralph's a cute little pup," said my father, gazing down at the dog, who was still sound asleep on the rug at my feet. "I have to say, he doesn't seem like he'll be much trouble at all."

"Well, we're going upstairs," my mother said. "I can't wait to get out of these high heels. Don't you girls stay up too late, though."

Before I could say anything, they were gone.

Randy, Katie, Sabs, and I looked at each other and burst out laughing.

"Quiet evening!" I said, still laughing. "That's a good one!"

"Really," said Randy, "tonight was about as quiet as a hurricane!"

"Oh, well," said Katie, "at least your parents didn't come home in the middle of it all."

"That's for sure," said Sabrina. "Somehow I don't think your mom and dad would have appreciated walking in with Barrett crying, the mess in the living room, and Ralph running all over the place."

I looked down at Ralph, who was still sleeping soundly on the rug. He must have been dreaming or something, because one of his hind legs kept twitching, as if he was running or something. Right then he looked so totally angelic that it was even easy for me to forget that he was the one who had caused all the trouble in the first place.

Chapter Six

The following Tuesday Billy Dixon and I met in school for our special weekly tutoring session. Tutoring is how Billy and I got to know each other. A while ago I volunteered to be a peer tutor and help a student who was having trouble with schoolwork. Billy was assigned to me.

It turned out that Billy was having so much trouble in school because he had a reading problem. Since then he's been going to a reading specialist every day. Billy and I got kind of used to working together, though, so we decided to turn our once-a-week tutoring session into a study session. We use that period to go over some of the work from our other classes, and it really helps both of us learn more.

I went to the classroom where we usually meet and sat down to wait for him. I took out my math book and put it on the desk in front of me. Although Billy has trouble reading, he's really incredible in math, and I planned to ask him for some help. I'm a good student, but math definitely isn't my favorite subject, especially now that we were doing all kinds of stuff with positive and negative numbers. Positive numbers are okay, of course, since they're just like regular numbers, but there's something about the idea of negative numbers that just doesn't seem to make sense to me. I mean, it's not like you can eat negative five apples, or read negative three books.

A few moments later Billy walked in. He was wearing a pair of worn, ripped jeans, and a really soft-looking, frayed blue-plaid flannel shirt.

"Hi, Allie," he said, putting his books down on the desk next to mine.

"Hi, Billy," I said, noticing how the blue of his plaid shirt really brought out the blue of his eyes.

"So what do you want to work on today?" he asked.

"Well, I could definitely use some help with this math," I told him. "How about you?"

"Math? No problem," he said, grinning and shaking a lock of his dark hair off his forehead. "What I'm having trouble with is this English essay we're supposed to write."

"Oh, I'll help you with that, Billy," I said.

English is my best subject. In fact, I had already started planning my own English essay a week ago.

"You've got a deal, Allie," he said, grinning at me. "I'll tell you what. Let's do some math first, and then we can work on the English."

I opened up my math book, and Billy and I began to work on some of the positive and negative number problems. After we had done a few together, it seemed to get a lot easier for me. Soon I was doing them on my own. Sometimes it really helps to have someone explain something to you a little differently from the way the teacher did.

After that I talked to Billy a little bit about his English essay. He definitely had some really good ideas, but he was having trouble organizing them. So I suggested he make an outline first before writing anything. I showed him how I usually make a list of all the points I want to write about, and then arrange them into groups, with an introduction and conclusion. He agreed that it was a good way to organize your ideas.

We finished up just as the bell rang for the end of the period.

"Wow, Allie, that was great," he said, closing his notebook. "I feel a whole lot better about this essay now."

"And I feel better about the math, too, thanks to you," I said, gathering up my things.

"Hey, by the way," he said as we headed toward the classroom door, "how's everything going with Charlie's dog?"

I rolled my eyes.

"Oh, you mean Ralph the maniac?" I asked.

Billy laughed.

"I had a feeling that puppy might turn out to be a little frisky," he said.

"I guess you might call chewing every shoe he can get his teeth on, going to the bathroom on the floor, and barking all the time *frisky*," I said, grinning.

"Wow," said Billy. "Sounds like a lot to handle."

"Actually, he seems to be finally calming down a little," I told him, pushing open the classroom door and stepping out into the hall. "But he still is a lot to handle. And I'm the one who's supposed to be teaching Charlie how to handle him. But I have to admit, Ralph's a cutie. And Charlie's totally in love with him. So I guess it's worth all the work."

Billy's face darkened.

"It is worth it, Allie," he said in a serious voice. "No matter how much trouble it is. I mean, if you could have seen —" He stopped speaking and was silent for a few seconds. "Let's just say Ralph's really lucky that your family took him out of that shelter and gave him a good home."

I looked at Billy closely. He definitely looked upset about something. Suddenly I remembered the funny look he had had on his face that day at the shelter, after he had gone to look for Miss Peabody.

"Billy, what is it?" I asked. "What's wrong?"

"Nothing, Allie," he said quickly. "I mean, forget it. There's nothing we can do about it anyway. Listen, I've got to run. I'm late for class."

And before I could say anything else, he took off down the hall.

I couldn't stop thinking about it all day, though. I just kept wondering what Billy wasn't telling me. Billy and I are really good friends, and it wasn't like him to keep a secret from me.

At the end of the day, as Sabs, Katie, Randy, and I were getting our things together at our lockers, Sabrina turned to me.

"So, Allie," she said, "how's cute little Ralph?"

"Really," asked Randy, pulling on her black

leather jacket, "is the cute little demon still tearing up the house?"

"Actually, he seems to have calmed down a little," I said, putting my books into my blue flowered backpack. "I think maybe he just had a lot of extra energy at first from being in that cage at the shelter for so long."

"I guess that makes sense, Allie," said Katie, zipping up her cream-colored corduroy jacket. "But don't you think they let them out sometimes to get some exercise?"

"I'm not sure," I said. "I mean, I didn't see any yards or anything, and the building itself was pretty small. There were a few other rooms I didn't get to see, though."

Suddenly I had a thought. Billy had seen what was in those other rooms! And it was right after that that he had come back with the funny look on his face. I wondered what he had seen that had made him so upset. I made up my mind right then and there to find out what it was that Billy had seen.

"Listen, you guys. There's something important I need to talk to Billy about," I said, quickly pulling on my jeans jacket.

"Billy Dixon?" asked Sabrina, looking up

from her book bag.

"What is it?" asked Katie.

"Is something wrong, Allie?" asked Randy.

"I can't talk now," I called, grabbing my bag and hurrying away. "I've got to catch him before he leaves school. I'll call you later!"

As I raced down the hall toward Billy's locker, I got a terrible feeling inside. I definitely had the idea that Billy knew something really bad about the shelter that he wasn't telling me.

"Billy! Billy!" I cried, running up to him so fast that I practically smashed into him in front of his locker.

"Allie, what is it?" he asked, taking me by the shoulders and looking concerned. "Are you okay?"

"Yes, yes," I panted. "I'm fine. It's just that —"

"What?" he said, looking at me.

I took a deep breath.

"Billy, I want you to tell me about the shelter," I said. "I know that something there upset you, and I want to know what it was."

Billy sighed.

"Oh, Allie," he said, shaking his head, "I should have known I couldn't keep that from you. But I thought it would just make you upset, too, if I told you. Besides, I figured we couldn't do anything about it anyway."

"Billy," I said, "whatever it is, I want to know."

He looked at me.

"It's just what I saw when I went to look for Miss Peabody," he said. "There were these other rooms filled with animals, but they were nothing like the room she had taken us to."

"What do you mean?" I asked.

"Well, first of all, the cages for the animals were a lot smaller than the ones in the room we were in," he explained. "I guess it was so that they could get more of them in. Some of the animals could barely move. And the rooms were incredibly overcrowded. There were dogs, cats, birds, and even rabbits in the same room, all barking or screaming — or whatever they do — at each other."

"Oh, Billy, how sad," I said.

"That's not all, Allie," he went on, looking really sad. "Some of the cages looked like they hadn't been cleaned out in days. And a lot of the food and water bowls were completely empty."

I couldn't believe what I was hearing.

"That's terrible!" I said, putting my hands up

to my face.

"Well, Allie," he said quietly, looking down at the floor, "now you know why I didn't want to tell you about it. And now you know why I said Ralph was so lucky to get adopted by you guys."

I felt like I was about to cry. The thought of all those poor animals living in such bad conditions really made me feel terrible.

But then I got an even worse thought. Suppose there was no money to keep the animals, and they had to be "put to sleep"!

"Billy," I said, "we have to do something!"

"What can we do, Allie?" he said. "It's just one of those things. It's really sad, but that's the way it is."

"Well, I can't just stand by and let this happen to all those animals," I said, clenching my fists angrily. "I may not know exactly what to do yet, but I do know I have to do something!"

Chapter Seven

Allison calls Randy.

RANDY: Hello?

ALLISON: Hi, Randy, it's me, Allison.

RANDY: Hi, what's up? You sure took off fast this afternoon.

ALLISON: Yes, well, that's sort of why I'm calling. It's about what Billy told me he'd seen at the Acorn Falls Animal Shelter.

RANDY: You mean the place you got Ralph? What about it?

ALLISON: Well, after Charlie had decided he wanted to take Ralph, Billy went to look for the woman in charge, Miss Peabody, so we could tell her. And while he was looking for her, he went into a couple of the other rooms in the shelter. Oh, Randy, what Billy says he saw in there sounds just horrible. There were a lot of other animals, all crowded together and locked up in cages so tiny they could hardly move.

RANDY: Wow, Al, that sounds really bad.

ALLISON: I know, isn't it terrible? Billy also said that the cages were really dirty, like they hadn't been cleaned out in days, and that a lot of the animals didn't even have food or water.

RANDY: What about the room you were in? Was it dirty, too?

ALLISON: No, that's just the thing. The Visitors' Room, where we were, had much bigger cages, and they were all completely clean. But you know, something happened when we first got to the shelter that seemed kind of funny to me.

RANDY: What?

ALLISON: When we got there, Miss Peabody told us to wait out in the reception room while she got things ready for us inside. I remember thinking it was strange. I mean, what would she have to get ready, and why couldn't we just go right in and see the animals the way they were?

RANDY: Well, I guess now you know. She probably had to get that Visitors' Room looking good enough for visitors. What a sad story.

ALLISON: It sure is. Now the only question is, what are we going to do about it?

RANDY: *Do* about it? What *can* we do about it?

ALLISON: Well, we just can't sit back and do nothing now that we know what's going on.

RANDY: Well, how about calling the police or something?

ALLISON: I thought of that, but all that would really do is get Miss Peabody in trouble. And as far as I can tell, she's the only person taking care of those animals at all. And I think she cares about them.

RANDY: But what about the way she's treating them? It sounds like they'd be a lot better off without her to me!

ALLISON: Well, if she weren't there, they

might just "put all the animals to sleep."

RANDY: That's awful, Al. But what do we do, adopt them all?

ALLISON: Actually, Randy, that might not be such a bad idea.

RANDY: Allison Cloud, I don't know about you, but I definitely can't take all those animals home. I mean, M's pretty cool, but somehow I don't think she'd be too understanding if I suddenly turned our house into Noah's Ark.

ALLISON: I know, I know. Believe me, it was hard enough convincing my parents to let us get Ralph. There's no way they'd let us get another pet. But there must be some people we know who'd be willing to adopt animals. Maybe we could talk to some of the kids at school or something.

RANDY: That sounds like a good idea.

ALLISON: I think I'll call Sabs and Katie and see what they think. I mean, maybe they know some people who might be willing to adopt pets.

RANDY: Sure, Al. I mean, it's worth a try, right? I guess I'll talk to you later.

ALLISON: Okay, Randy. Bye.

Allison calls Sabrina.

SABRINA: Hello. Wells residence.

ALLISON: Hi, Sabs, it's me, Allie.

SABRINA: Oh, hi.

ALLISON: Listen, Sabs, I have something to tell you. When we were at the animal shelter on Saturday, Billy went into some of the back rooms and saw some animals being kept in pretty bad conditions.

SABRINA: Oh, gosh, I hate hearing about stuff like this. It makes me feel so sad.

ALLISON: I know, me too. Which is exactly why we've got to do something about it.

SABRINA: Okay, count me in. But what are we going to do?

ALLISON: Well, the shelter is really overcrowded. There isn't enough room for all the animals to live comfortably, and there aren't enough people to take care of them properly. The way I see it, our only hope is to convince as many people as possible to adopt pets from the shelter.

SABRINA: That sounds like a good idea. And it shouldn't be too hard. I mean, everybody likes animals, right? Who can resist a furry face?

ALLISON: Wait a minute, Sabs — say that again!

SABRINA: What? All I said was "Who can resist —"

ALLISON: "— a furry face." Right! I knew it sounded familiar. That's it — we've found the answer!

SABRINA: Al, what are you talking about?

ALLISON: Sabs, do you remember the last time you said that? It was at lunch last week, and we were talking about endangered species.

SABRINA: Oh, yeah, that's right. We were trying to figure out what S.A.F.E.'s next project should be.

ALLISON: So, don't you see? We have the answer. I mean, now we have endangered animals right here in Acorn Falls that need our help.

SABRINA: Oh, I get it! You're saying that S.A.F.E. should take on the Acorn Falls Animal Shelter as its next project.

ALLISON: That's right. The way I see it, with all the members of S.A.F.E. working together, we should be able to spread the word about the situation at the shelter pretty quickly.

SABRINA: That's a great idea, Allie.

ALLISON: I think so, too. Our next meeting is the day after tomorrow. I guess I'll bring up the idea then and see what everybody thinks.

SABRINA: Oh, I'm sure it'll go over really well. I mean, helping animals is a really good cause.

ALLISON: Okay, listen, Sabs. I was going to call Katie and tell her about the problem, but now that we have a solution, I think I should call Randy back and let her know. After all, I was pretty upset when I talked to her a minute ago, and I'd kind of like to reassure her.

SABRINA: Okay, you go ahead and call

	Randy. Meanwhile I'll call Katie and tell her everything.
ALLISON:	Great, Sabs. Thanks.
SABRINA:	Okay, bye, Allie.
ALLISON:	Bye.

Sabrina calls Katie.

KATIE:	Hello. Beauvais and Campbell residence.
SABRINA:	Hi, Katie, it's Sabrina.
KATIE:	Oh, hi, Sabrina.
SABRINA:	Listen, I just got off the phone with Allie, and it looks like she's got a really great idea for the next S.A.F.E. project.
KATIE:	Oh, good, what is it?
SABRINA:	Well, Allie found out that the Acorn Falls Animal Shelter is really overcrowded, and that because of it, a lot of the animals there aren't being taken care of very well.
KATIE:	Oh, that's terrible.
SABRINA:	So anyway, she got to thinking about it, and she realized that it might be a good idea to get S.A.F.E. involved.

KATIE: That sounds great, but how?

SABRINA: You know, to have S.A.F.E. members spread the word and get people to adopt animals.

KATIE: What a fantastic idea, Sabrina! I'm sure that will help a lot.

SABRINA: That's what I said. Anyway, Allie's going to talk about it at the next S.A.F.E. meeting.

KATIE: Great, Sabs. Thanks for letting me know about it.

SABRINA: Sure, Katie. I'll see you in school tomorrow.

KATIE: Okay, Sabs. Bye.

Allison calls Randy.

RANDY: Hello?

ALLISON: Hi, Randy.

RANDY: Hi, Allie.

ALLISON: Listen, I just got off the phone with Sabs, and I think I have a good idea for how to get people to adopt animals from the shelter.

RANDY: Cool. What is it?

ALLISON: Well, Sabs mentioned something that reminded me about how I had

	been thinking of getting S.A.F.E. involved in something to do with endangered species for our next project.
RANDY:	Sure, I remember.
ALLISON:	Well, anyway, I started thinking it might be a good idea to get S.A.F.E. involved in helping the shelter animals.
RANDY:	You mean get S.A.F.E. members to talk to people about adopting pets from the shelter?
ALLISON:	That's right. What do you think?
RANDY:	That's an incredible idea, Allie! I bet that will really make a big difference.
ALLISON:	I hope so. Anyway, I guess I'll bring it up at the S.A.F.E. meeting on Thursday.
RANDY:	Cool, Allie. Thanks for calling me back to tell me about it.
ALLISON:	Okay, Randy. I guess I'll see you tomorrow in school.
RANDY:	All right, Al, *Ciao!*

Chapter Eight

At the end of the school day on Thursday, two days after my phone conversations with my friends, I headed down the hall at Bradley toward the classroom where we usually hold our S.A.F.E. meetings. I was wearing a cropped, hooded pink zip-front sweatshirt with a gathered pink-and-black polka-dot miniskirt, pale-pink tights, and black flats. My long black hair was in a high ponytail with a pink scrunchy, and my green spiral notebook for S.A.F.E. records was under one arm.

As I walked into the classroom, I was amazed to see that, instead of the usual ten or fifteen kids who showed up at our meetings, the classroom was practically overflowing with people. There were a bunch of kids there that I didn't even know, but I did recognize Alex Selby, the eighth grader that Randy and I had spoken to in the lunchroom. I figured that he must have told his friends about the meeting.

The kids were talking a lot, but as I took my place in the front of the room, they became completely quiet. Everybody was looking right at me. I opened my green spiral notebook and put it on the desk. I couldn't help feeling a little nervous. After all, it was definitely the biggest turnout we had ever had for a S.A.F.E. meeting, and I knew it was up to me to start the meeting. I also knew that what I had to tell them about today was really important. The future of the animals at the Acorn Falls Animal Shelter was up to me!

"Hi, everybody," I said, looking around the room and managing a smile. "I'd like to thank you all for coming, and to welcome those of you who are here for the first time today. My name is Allison Cloud."

I glanced at Randy, who was sitting on one of the windowsills on the right, and she winked at me and gave me the thumbs-up sign.

I started by telling them something about the background of S.A.F.E., and how I had decided to start the club in order to make students more aware of the problems facing our environment. Then I explained a little bit about the monthly recycling program, and how it worked. By that time I was feeling a whole lot more relaxed. After all, I thought to myself, everyone was there for the same reason I was, to do what they could to make the planet a better place to live.

"S.A.F.E.'s recycling program has been really successful," I told them. "Since we started the program, we've almost doubled the amount of newspapers, cans, and bottles we send to the recycling program each month. And that's mostly because we've been able to get the word out at Bradley. Teachers and students here are starting to realize how important it is to get involved."

I looked at Alex, and he grinned back at me.

"But now there's something else I'd like to ask you all to get involved in," I went on. I took a deep breath. "One of our members has discovered a serious problem at the Acorn Falls Animal Shelter."

I saw Billy look at me and nod his head slowly.

"The shelter is really overcrowded," I said, looking around the room at everyone, "and, because of it, a lot of the animals that live there are suffering. The conditions there are really bad. Some of the animals are in cages so small, they can hardly move. And the cages aren't even cleaned regularly. On top of that, a lot of the animals don't get enough food and water."

I heard someone gasp.

"I know this is really upsetting to hear," I said. "But I'm telling you about it not just to upset you. What I'm hoping is that S.A.F.E. can try to make a difference. Miss Peabody, who runs the shelter, doesn't seem to have enough help or enough money to do all she should. And since the whole idea of the club is to try to make the planet a better place for everyone, that includes animals, too. The way I see it, now that we know what's going on over at the shelter, it's our responsibility to try to do something about it."

A girl near the front spoke up.

"But what can we do about it?" she said with a concerned look on her face. "I mean, it sounds like someone has to do something to help those animals. But, after all, we're just kids, right? How much of a difference can we really make?"

"If there's one thing that S.A.F.E.'s taught me, it's that kids can make a difference when we see something wrong," I told her firmly. "Especially if we get together and get organized. And as far as I'm concerned, we owe it to the animals to try to help them out."

Suddenly I had pictures in my mind of Ralph — of how he wagged his tail the minute you even looked at him, of how he loved to be picked up and held, and of how he was always trying to lick Charlie's face.

"I mean, the great thing about animals is that they love you no matter what," I said. "My family adopted a dog from the shelter, and you can just tell how happy he is to have a family to love now. I'm sure all of those animals at the shelter would make great pets. But right now they're all just innocent victims. It's not their fault that the shelter is overcrowded, and it's not like they can even speak up for themselves. Which is why it's up to us to speak for them."

"You're right, Allie," said Billy, looking right at me. "It is our responsibility to try to change things at the shelter."

I smiled back at him. I was really glad that Billy had said that, because it meant he wasn't sorry that he had told me about the shelter in the first place.

Then Arizonna, this really nice guy in our class who used to live in California, nodded.

"Count me in," he said. "It's definitely time for us humans to get it into our heads that we're not the only living things on the planet. So, what do you want us to do, Allison?"

"Well," I said, "I think the best thing we can do for the shelter is to try to get people to adopt as many of the pets as possible. I've been thinking about it, and my idea is to organize some kind of adopt-a-pet day to make people aware that there are lots of great animals available at the shelter."

"That's a really good idea," said Mary Engle, a girl I knew from gym class. "We could make posters and stuff and put them up around school."

"Yes," I said, "posters would definitely be good. And I think we should try to take this campaign outside of school, too. We definitely need to spread the word to as many people as we can if we really want to help the animals."

"Well, how about putting up posters all around Acorn Falls, too?" suggested Katie, tucking a lock of her silky blond hair behind one ear.

"I'm sure my father would let us put one in the window of his hardware store," exclaimed Sabrina excitedly.

"And my parents own Town and Country Fabrics over on Guilford Lane," called another girl from the back. "We could put a poster there, too."

"Hey, how about passing out fliers?" suggested Randy. "You know, they could say something like 'Pick a great pet at the Acorn Falls Animal Shelter.'"

"That's it," I said, grinning. "That's what we'll call it — 'Acorn Falls Pick-a-Pet Day.'"

"Yeah," said Alex, nodding. "'Pick-a-Pet,' that's kind of catchy."

"But I definitely think we should get started on this right away," I said. "I say we set Pick-a-Pet Day for a week from this Saturday."

"Wow," said Arizonna, "that doesn't give us much time."

"I know," I said, "but I think it's really important to get help to those animals as soon as possible. Besides, I believe we can do it if we really get organized. For example, maybe we can try to get together a few poster-painting groups this weekend for anyone who has time to volunteer. And one thing we can all start to do right away is to try to tell as many people about Pick-a-Pet Day as we can. So, everybody here, please talk to your friends about it, talk to your parents about it, even talk to your parents' friends about it — just get the word out. Meanwhile I'll try to have some fliers available by Monday, so anyone who wants to pass them out can stop by here after school and get some from me."

"What about this Miss Peabody who runs the shelter?" asked Arizonna. "Shouldn't somebody tell her? She won't know what hit her."

I hadn't thought of that. Arizonna was right.

"I'll tell her," Billy called out. "I'm sure she'll be very happy to hear about Pick-a-Pet Day."

"Thanks, Billy," I said. "That's a big help."

I looked at my watch. It was almost four o'clock. The meeting had been going on for forty-five minutes, and I knew that some of the kids must be anxious to leave now.

"Okay," I said, "that's the end of today's meeting. Thanks a lot for coming, and I hope I didn't keep you too late. Anyone interested in organizing a poster-painting group or helping out in some other way, just let me know."

To my surprise, hardly anyone left the room. As a matter of fact, in a couple of seconds, I was completely surrounded by kids volunteering to help out. There were kids offering to paint posters, hand out fliers, and pass the word out through clubs and groups they belonged to outside of school. I was amazed. But I guessed Sabs was right — maybe it was true that no one could resist a furry face. Whatever the reason, it made me feel really great to know that so many kids cared enough about the animals to help.

Chapter Nine

"Okay, Allie!" called Randy, banging up the back steps to my room. "We're here! Where do you want all this stuff?"

"I brought some newspapers," said Katie, coming up the steps behind her. "I thought maybe that would help keep things from getting too messy."

It was Saturday, two days after the big S.A.F.E. meeting. Randy, Katie, Sabrina, and I had decided to organize a poster-painting group at my house. We also planned to design a flier so we could get some copies made and have them ready to pass out by Monday afternoon.

"Hi, guys," I said, jumping up to open my french door for them. "Newspapers — that's great, Katie. I looked around for some here, but I must have already bundled them all and taken them to school for the recycling drive."

"You mean to tell me that there isn't one

newspaper in your whole house?" asked Randy, putting down the shopping bag she was carrying and sitting on my bed. "Wow, you don't waste a second, do you, Allie?"

I shrugged.

"I guess I am a little extra-enthusiastic when it comes to recycling," I admitted. "Sometimes I end up bundling the newspapers before my parents are even done reading them."

"It's a good thing you don't live in my house," said Katie, pulling off her denim jacket with the light-blue flowered cotton sleeves. "My mother likes to do the crossword puzzle, and she gets pretty upset if anyone throws out the paper before she's done with it."

I looked into the bag that Randy had put on the floor. It was filled with paint and brushes.

"Wow, this stuff looks great, Randy," I said.

"Yeah, once I told M about the animals and everything, she said I could take as much stuff from her studio as I needed," said Randy.

"M" is what Randy calls her mother. Olivia, which is what the rest of us call her, is an artist. She has a big studio filled with art supplies in the converted barn where she and Randy live.

Katie looked around.

"Where's Sabs?" she asked. "Wasn't she going to try to get here early to help us set up?"

"She just called a little while ago," I said. "She's trying to talk Luke into letting her bring his camera."

Luke is one of Sabrina's brothers. He's never exactly eager to do Sabs favors, and he's especially possessive about his camera, which his grandmother gave him for Christmas. Sabs actually did get him to lend it to us once before, so the two of us could take pictures of each other to send in with our applications for the Junior Miss Acorn Falls Pageant, but she had had to promise to do his chores for a week to get him to agree to it.

"But what do we need a camera for?" asked Randy.

"Well, I thought maybe we could take a picture of Ralph and try to use it on the flier," I told them. "If we take it to that one-hour photo place on Main Street, it'll be developed in time to have the fliers ready for Monday."

"That's a great idea," said Katie.

"A photograph will definitely make the flier more eye-catching," agreed Randy.

"That's what I thought," I said. "Besides, it kind of seemed appropriate, since Ralph was once a shelter dog, too."

Just then we heard someone clumping up the back steps to my room.

"Hi, I'm here!" called Sabrina, appearing on my terrace in a pair of pink cropped pants and a short white cotton jacket.

"Hi, Sabs," I said, standing up again to let her in.

"Hi, Sabrina," called Randy and Katie.

"Oh, good," I said, noticing the camera in her hand. "You brought it."

"Yeah," she said, grinning, as she came inside. "I finally talked Luke into it."

"Boy, Sabrina," said Randy. "I hate to think of the deal you had to make with Luke to get it."

Sabrina giggled.

"Actually, it was just the opposite," she said. "I suddenly started thinking that Luke has always had a really soft spot in his heart for Cinnamon, our dog. He likes to act tough sometimes, but I know it's always Luke who gives Cin scraps from the table and brushes and bathes her. So I decided to tell him about the shelter. I figured he might lend us the camera if he knew it would help the animals."

"And?" asked Katie. "It worked?"

"It sure did." Sabrina beamed. "By the time I was finished describing the conditions at the shelter, Luke had not only given me his camera, but had promised to help out by spreading the word over at the high school about the animals, too. In fact, he told me to make sure to get a bunch of fliers from you, Allie."

"Wow, Sabrina, that's incredible!" I exclaimed.

"Really," said Randy. "Who'd have guessed Luke was such a softie after all?"

"I guess there's just something about the idea of helping animals that really makes people want to work together," said Katie.

"Speaking of working together," I said, looking at the clock on my night table, "the other kids are going to be here pretty soon. Maybe we should go take that picture of Ralph so we can get the poster stuff set up here before they arrive."

"Sounds good to me, Allie," said Randy, standing up.

"Where is Ralph anyway?" asked Sabs.

"He's down in the garden with Charlie," I said. "In fact, I thought that might be a good place to take his picture."

Pulling on our jackets, we headed out onto my terrace and down the back steps to the garden, where Charlie and Ralph were playing a game of fetch together.

"Aw, how cute," said Sabrina.

"Wow, Ralph's really learning to fetch," said Randy.

I had to admit, it made me feel kind of warm inside to see Charlie and Ralph playing there so happily. But then, as we got closer, I saw what Charlie was having Ralph fetch and bring back to him — a pair of neatly rolled-up socks, no doubt straight from the clean laundry basket I had seen my mother organizing earlier.

"Charlie!" I called. "What are you doing? Whose socks are those?"

Charlie looked at the socks in his hands and shrugged.

"Grandpa's, I guess," he said.

"I'm telling you, that dog just can't keep away from footwear," Randy joked.

I sighed.

"Charlie," I said carefully, "Ralph has plenty of toys of his own. You shouldn't let him chew Grandpa's socks."

"Oh," said Charlie sheepishly. "Okay. Sorry, Ralph. You're not supposed to chew these. It isn't 'sponsible."

He held the balled-up socks above his head, where Ralph couldn't reach them. But that only made Ralph — who didn't understand why this new toy was suddenly being taken away from him — start running in circles around Charlie, barking loudly and wagging his tail.

"Here, Ralph!" I called, spotting a red rubber ball lying in the grass. "Here, Ralphie. You play with this."

I picked up the ball and held it up for him to see. He looked at me, but he couldn't have cared less about the ball. All he wanted were those socks in Charlie's hands.

"Charlie, hide the socks so he'll forget about them," suggested Sabrina.

Charlie looked around, with Ralph dancing around him and barking wildly. Finally he stuffed the socks down the front of his jeans jacket.

"Here, Ralph!" I called again, holding up the red rubber ball. "Here, boy. Here's your toy!"

"Go get it, Ralph," urged Katie.

"It's no use," said Sabrina as Ralph completely ignored me and leaped wildly at Charlie's chest, trying to get at the socks inside his jacket.

"Well, I guess it's a good thing I wore old sneakers today," muttered Randy, suddenly bending down to untie one of her worn black high-tops.

"Randy, what are you doing?" I asked.

"I told you," she said, looking up at me and grinning, "this dog of yours is only interested in footwear. Now watch this."

She let out a long whistle, and Ralph suddenly snapped to attention.

"Here you go, Ralph. Try this on for size," she said, tossing her sneaker onto the grass.

Ralph sprang into action, running over to Randy's sneaker and snatching it in his mouth. He carried it to a corner of the garden and settled down with the sneaker in his mouth.

"Well," said Randy, beaming, "there's your picture. Just hurry up and take it before he devours my entire sneaker, okay?"

"Wow," said Charlie, wide-eyed, "how'd you do that?"

"Randy, you are unbelievable," I said, laughing.

"Smile and say 'Cheese,' Ralph," said Sabs, crouching down in front of him with the camera.

"I don't know, you guys," said Katie. "Do we really want to put a picture on the flier of a dog chewing a sneaker? I mean, doesn't it kind of give the rest of the shelter animals a bad reputation?"

"That's a really good point, Katie," I said. "We don't want people to think they're going to lose their shoes to a dog they adopt from the shelter."

"But Ralph's not going to stay put if we take away the sneaker," said Sabrina, still crouched behind the camera.

"That's true," said Katie. "And he looks so good there in the grass."

"I have an idea," I said. "Randy, he definitely noticed your whistle before. Maybe if you do it again, he'll look up and stop chewing the sneaker. If Sabs takes the picture right then, we can cut off the bottom of the picture, the part with the sneaker in it."

"Okay, sounds good to me," said Randy, positioning herself right above Sabrina. "Get that shutter finger ready, Sabs."

"Okay, Randy," said Sabs. "Go ahead."

Randy let out a long whistle, and just like before, Ralph looked right up at her. But this time he dropped the sneaker. It only lasted a few seconds, though.

"I think I got it," said Sabrina from behind the camera. "But I'm not sure."

"You should probably take a few pictures, just

to be safe," I suggested.

After a few more whistles, and a few more breaks in Ralph's sneaker chewing, Sabs was satisfied that she had gotten a good picture. Getting Randy's sneaker back from Ralph wasn't quite so easy, though. Every time one of us tried to grab it, he would run away with it in his mouth. Once Katie actually managed to get hold of it, but Ralph thought she was playing tug-of-war. He just sank his teeth more deeply into it, matching every one of Katie's tugs with one of his own.

Finally I had to give in and tell Charlie to take my grandfather's socks back out of his jacket. It worked. Ralph pounced on them happily as soon as he saw them, completely abandoning Randy's sneaker. But I couldn't help feeling like it wasn't really the best thing to do. Not that my grandfather would actually miss that pair of socks. After all, he had a whole drawerful of them. But we didn't exactly seem to be breaking Ralph of his footwear habit.

Randy, Katie, Sabs, and I headed back up to my room to set up for the poster painting, leaving Charlie and Ralph to play with their socks in the garden. Ten minutes later we had pushed back all my furniture and spread newspaper all over my floor. We were just finishing putting out the poster board, paint, and brushes when the other kids began to arrive.

"Wow!" said Arizonna, coming up the back steps and looking around. "Extremely excellent pad, Allison Cloud."

I grinned. Arizonna definitely has an unusual way of saying things.

"Come on in, Arizonna," I said, handing him a paintbrush.

A few minutes later my room was filled with kids painting posters. In addition to Arizonna, there were Sabrina's twin brother, Sam; Sam's two best friends, Nick and Jason; Billy; Alex and a couple of his friends; and three other girls from the seventh grade who had been attending the S.A.F.E. meetings lately.

It made me feel really great that so many kids had volunteered to help out. We worked hard, and we all had fun, too. By the time we were done, we had made over thirty posters advertising Pick-a-Pet Day. As we were putting the finishing touches on them, there was a knock on the door that leads from my room to the upstairs hall.

"Allie, it's me!" Charlie called. "Nooma said to bring you all a snack, but I can't open the door with this tray in my hands."

"I'll get it," Billy volunteered, putting down the brush he was holding and carefully stepping over the wet posters spread all over the floor. "Hey, Charlie, how are you doing? Come on in."

But unfortunately, as Billy opened the door, Ralph, who must have followed Charlie upstairs, came bounding into the room.

"Oh, no!" I cried, a wet paintbrush in my hand. "Stop him, quick!"

But before anyone could do anything, Ralph had run in one big circle on top of the wet posters, leaving pawprints of wet paint all over them.

"Uh-oh," said Charlie, who was still standing in the doorway with the tray in his hands. "I think maybe Ralph forgot to be 'sponsible again."

Somehow Sam managed to catch up with Ralph and grab him before he could do too much more damage. Billy wiped the paint off Ralph's paws with an old rag, and I grabbed Ralph and held him on my lap.

Charlie served the oatmeal cookies and lemonade as I held the squirming puppy. I looked down at the pawprint-covered posters and shook my head. No doubt about it — Ralph had done it again. This was sure going to be tough to clean up.

But then I had a thought.

"Hey," I said suddenly. "Maybe we should leave them like that."

"What?" asked Randy, taking a sip of her lemonade. "You mean the posters?"

"Sure," I said, holding my cookie away from Ralph, who was trying to take a bite of it. "Let's leave the pawprints there. I mean, after all, the posters are supposed to advertise animals, right?"

"Oh, I get it," said Sam, munching on another cookie.

"They do look kind of cute," said Katie.

I looked down at Ralph.

"Well, demon doggie," I said, putting my face near his, "I guess you're going to get away with this, after all."

Ralph, who was looking right back up at me, suddenly planted a huge wet kiss on my nose, and everybody burst into laughter.

Chapter Ten

The next week we were really busy getting ready for Pick-a-Pet Day. Fortunately, Mary Birdsong came back from Chicago, so at least I didn't have to take care of Charlie and Barrett at all.

Randy had finished the flier over the weekend, using a picture Sabs had taken, and it looked great. In the middle of the page was a photograph of Ralph looking right up at the camera — with no sign at all of the sneaker he had been chewing. Above it were written the words A FURRY FRIEND NEEDS YOUR HELP. COME ADOPT YOUR BEST FRIEND ON ACORN FALLS PICK-A-PET DAY. Underneath the picture were the date and the address of the shelter.

We were able to run off copies of the flier at school on Monday, and tons of kids showed up after school to get fliers to hand out. By Tuesday all of Bradley Junior High was talking about Pick-

a-Pet Day. Sabrina passed on a bunch of fliers to
Luke to hand out at the high school, and I even
gave some to Mary to take to Acorn Falls
Community College, and some to Charlie to pass
out at his elementary school. It was really cute to
see how proud Charlie was of Ralph's picture on
the fliers I gave him. He kept saying that now
Ralph was "famous."

Since our goal was to get the fliers out to as
many people as possible, I made sure I was never
without a bunch of them in my book bag.

On Tuesday I went to my Synchronized
Swimming Club meeting at the Acorn Falls
YWCA. Synchronized swimming is like a combi-
nation of dance or gymnastics and swimming.
I've been in the club a little while now, and it's
lots of fun. Since a lot of the kids in the club go to
other schools, I made sure to give a bunch of fliers
to each of them to pass out. And my synchronized swimming partner, Tory Wickers, promised
to take some to her father to pass out at his elec-
tronics store at the Widmere Mall.

On Wednesday, three days before Pick-a-Pet
Day, Randy, Katie, Sabrina, and I all decided to
head over to Main Street after school to hand out
fliers to store owners. Sabrina's father had

already been putting them in all his customers' bags at his hardware store, and we figured we could probably get a few more store owners to do the same thing.

We went to Book Soup first. Book Soup is this really great old used-book store on Main Street. It's one of my favorite places in all of Acorn Falls, and the owner, Max Dalton, is this really sweet elderly man. Once he almost had to close up the store, but Randy, Katie, Sabs, and I were able to help him stay in business.

After Book Soup we dropped off some fliers at the Main Street Theater, Fanciful Cards and Gifts, Andersen's Bakery, and Fun-Time Toys. Everybody we talked to in the shops was really enthusiastic about Pick-a-Pet Day, and they all promised to hand out the fliers to all their customers.

"Well, I'd call that a success," said Randy as the four of us stood on the corner of Main and Grand.

"Really," said Sabrina, "I bet everyone in this whole town's going to know about Pick-a-Pet Day by Saturday."

Glancing across the street, I suddenly said, "Hey, look at that!"

"*Acorn Falls Gazette?*" Randy read from the sign on the window. "So?"

"So," I said, heading across the street, "something tells me that the office of our town's newspaper might not be a bad place to take our fliers. Come on."

Randy, Katie, and Sabrina followed me across the street, and I pushed open the big glass door. Behind a counter stood a short bald man wearing little half-glasses, rearranging some papers in front of him.

"I'm sorry, girls," he said, looking up at us, "but if you're looking to buy the paper, you'll have to go down to the news shop on the corner. We just print it here. We don't sell it."

"Actually," I said, stepping forward, "it's the printing of the paper we wanted to talk to you about."

"Oh?" he said, raising his eyebrows and smiling.

"Yes," I went on. "We'd like to know if you'd be interested in printing a copy of our flier in the paper."

I took one of the fliers out of my bag and held it out to him.

"Ah, yes, you mean you want to take out an

advertisement," he said, without even looking at the flier. "Well, the rates are one hundred dollars for a half page —"

"A hundred dollars!" Sabrina burst out.

"Yes, that's right," the man said, going back to the papers on his desk. "But that's for a half-page only. If you want a full page, it'll be two hundred dollars."

"Excuse me, sir," I said, clearing my throat, "but this is sort of a special case. I mean, it's not exactly an ad we want you to print. Maybe if you take a look at it, you'll see what I mean."

The man looked up from his work again and I handed him the flier.

"Hmm," he said, reading it over. "'Pick-a-Pet Day,' eh? Over at the animal shelter?"

"That's right," I said. "You see, the shelter is really overcrowded, and we're trying to get people to adopt as many of the animals as possible. So, you see, it's not actually like a real ad for a store or something."

"Things at the shelter are really bad," said Katie behind me. "The animals really need our help."

"Well, you girls are in luck," said the man, smiling at us. "I'm Larry Mullen, the editor of the paper, and I agree with you. This is a very special situation indeed."

"We definitely think so, Mr. Mullen," I said.

"Which is why I've decided to print a copy of this flier in the paper at no charge," he told us.

"Really?" said Sabs. "That's great!"

"Hey, that's a really cool thing of you to do," said Randy. "Thanks."

"Now, I can't afford to give it a full page," he went on, "but I will do a half-page every day between now and Saturday."

"Thank you so much, Mr. Mullen," I said happily. "We really appreciate it."

"No problem at all," he said, putting the flier on the counter in front of him. "I'm happy to do it. I've always been rather fond of animals myself. Why, when I was a little boy, we had a rabbit hutch in our backyard with a big old fat white rabbit in it. Tiny was his name. I really loved that rabbit. Well, anyway, you girls look out for the ad in tomorrow's *Gazette*."

"We will," I called as we walked out. "And thanks again, Mr. Mullen."

Out on the street, Randy turned to me.

"That was totally cool, Allie," she said.

"Really," added Katie. "It'll be great publicity

for Pick-a-Pet Day."

"It sure will," said Sabrina. "Everybody in Acorn Falls reads the *Gazette*."

"Well, let's hope they all come to the shelter on Saturday, too," I said.

Chapter Eleven

"Ohmygosh — look at this!" exclaimed Sabrina excitedly, pointing at the line of cars parked along Dillard Street.

It was Saturday morning, Acorn Falls Pick-a-Pet Day, and Randy, Katie, Sabs, and I were walking up Dillard Street toward the Acorn Falls Animal Shelter.

Just then a little girl skipped by. She was holding her father's hand with one of hers, and in the other she had a piece of rope that was tied around the neck of a big fluffy sheepdog. The dog was almost as big as the little girl, and it was wagging its tail happily.

"Oh, Daddy," the girl said excitedly, skipping to keep up with the big dog, "wait till Mommy sees Fuzzy. She's just gonna love him!"

"Aw," said Katie, "isn't that cute? I guess they just adopted that dog."

"I bet Fuzzy was pretty happy to get out of

his cage," said Randy. "He sure doesn't look like the type of dog that would be comfortable in a small space."

The closer we got to the shelter, the more people we saw with animals. There were dogs, cats — even birds. One old man walked by us holding his hat upside-down, with three tiny gray kittens sitting inside.

"Wow," said Sabs. "This is incredible. I wonder what's going on inside."

"Come on," I said. "Let's go in."

We hurried up the steps and made our way in past the reception room. As we walked down the hall, I was happy to see that all the doors that had been closed the last time I was here were open now and that tons of people were crowding into all the rooms.

"I bet the whole town will be here today," said Sabrina.

"Oh," said Katie, bending down to look at a kitten in one of the cages. "This one looks just like Pepper used to when I first got her."

"Ooooh, look at these two puppies," said Sabrina, hurrying over to another cage. "They're wrestling with each other."

"Wow," said Randy, looking into another, "look

at this cool bird."

Just then I noticed Billy Dixon walk out of the room directly across the hall. A cute little yellow puppy was asleep in his arms.

"Hi, Billy," I said, stepping out into the hall. "Looks like you've got a new friend there."

"Hi, Allie!" he said, grinning. "Yeah, I figured maybe it was about time we had another dog around my house."

"That's great, Billy," I said, petting the soft yellow fur of the puppy's head.

"This whole thing's great," said Billy, looking around. "Look at all these people. And Miss Peabody's so happy. Well, I'd better get this little guy home. I'll see you in school on Monday, okay?"

"Okay, Billy, bye-bye," I said, turning around to look for Sabrina, Randy, and Katie.

I found the three of them clustered around a cage in the corner. I couldn't see what it was they were looking at, but I could hear their voices as I made my way over to them.

"Aaaw, he's so sweet," Sabrina was saying.

"Are you really going to, Randy?" asked Katie.

"Hey, Allie," said Randy as I walked up to the three of them. She pointed at the cage. "Well, what do you think?"

I looked into the cage, where a tiny black kitten with a white diamond-shaped mark on its forehead was batting around a wad of newspaper with its paw.

"I think I'm going to name him Buddy," said Randy, grinning. "After Buddy Rich, my favorite drummer."

"You're kidding, Randy!" I said, excited. "You're getting a kitten?"

"Yeah, well, M and I talked it over this morning," she said. "And we agreed that we might be ready to take on a new member of the family."

"That's great, Randy," I said, looking at the kitten. "He's adorable."

"I know," said Randy, beaming. "And I really dig his black outfit, you know?"

We all laughed.

Just then I saw Miss Peabody making her way toward us through the crowded room with Mr. Mullen from the *Acorn Falls Gazette* and another woman I didn't recognize close behind her.

"Are these the girls you were telling me about, Mr. Mullen?" Miss Peabody asked, stopping in front of us.

"That's right," said Mr. Mullen. "Hello, everyone. I was just telling Miss Peabody here that she has you to thank for organizing the great turnout here today."

"How can I ever thank you?" said Miss Peabody, her eyes suddenly filling with tears. "It seems like forever that I've been struggling along here, trying to take care of all these animals by myself. It broke my heart to have to keep them cooped up like that, but there just wasn't enough money to build bigger facilities or to hire anyone to help me out. But now, thank goodness, all that has changed."

"You mean all the animals have been adopted?" I asked, amazed.

"Well, almost," she answered. "But it's more than that. Thanks to all the publicity, donations have been flowing in all day. Why, one wealthy businesswoman in the community has even offered to buy the empty lot next door so we can turn it into an exercise yard."

"That's great!" said Sabrina. "Now the animals won't have to stay cooped up anymore."

"Now I'd like to have my photographer here take a picture of you four, please," said Mr. Mullen.

The woman with him stepped forward and pointed a camera at Randy, Katie, Sabs, and me. Before any of us could say anything, there was a flash.

"Thank you, girls," said Mr. Mullen. "That picture's going on the front page of tomorrow's *Gazette*. Now, Miss Peabody, I'd like to see what you have in the way of rabbits. I'm looking for a big white one in particular. You know, I used to have one as a boy...."

Mr. Mullen's voice faded as he, Miss Peabody, and the photographer walked away.

"Ohmygosh!" said Sabrina excitedly. "Did you hear what he said? Our picture's going to be on the front page of the paper!"

"And it sounds like the shelter's really going to get fixed up," said Katie.

"Wow," said Randy. "I guess you could say that Pick-a-Pet Day was a pretty big success, huh?"

As I looked around at all the people peering into the cages and at all the animals that were getting good homes, I had to admit I felt pretty proud of what I had done. But mostly I was just glad I had been able to help.

Don't Miss
GIRL TALK #39
KATIE AND THE IMPOSSIBLE COUSINS

As I walked into the foyer of my house, I heard voices in the library. I walked across the polished wood floor and through the sliding oak doors that led into the library. Mom, Jean-Paul, Emily, and Michel were all talking excitedly. They didn't even notice me in the doorway.

"What's up?" I asked. Usually only Jean-Paul uses this room, since it's attached to his home office.

"Papa just got a phone call in his office from my uncle. My Grand-mère, my cousin Noelle, and my Tante Anne and Oncle Pierre are coming for a week's holiday!" Michel announced happily. He still talks with a thick French-Canadian accent, just like his father does.

Jean-Paul owns the biggest advertising company in Canada, and his brother-in-law — that's Oncle Pierre — runs the Canadian office. Jean-Paul runs the Minneapolis office, which is why he moved here to Acorn Falls.

Emily said, "I think I remember Tante Anne and Oncle Pierre from the wedding. She was wearing a really beautiful long blue chiffon gown and a sapphire necklace." Trust my sister, Emily, to remember in detail what everybody wore, I thought. "But did we meet cousin Noelle at the wedding?" she asked. "I can't remember her."

"No, she was away at boarding school in Switzerland and couldn't make it," Jean-Paul explained.

Boarding school in Switzerland! I figured she had to be practically grown-up if her parents let her go to school so far away. "How old is she?" I asked.

"That's the best part — Cousin Noelle is our age!" Michel told me happily. "And she's really nice, too."

"Great! I can't wait to meet her!" I said, trying to sound sincere. But I couldn't help wondering what I could possibly have in common with this girl.

TALK BACK!
TELL US WHAT YOU THINK ABOUT
GIRL TALK BOOKS

Name _____

Address _____

City _____ State _____ Zip_____

Birthday _____ Mo._____ Year _____

Telephone Number (____)_____

1) Did you like this GIRL TALK book?

Check one: YES_____ NO_____

2) Would you buy another GIRL TALK book?

Check one: YES_____ NO_____

If you like GIRL TALK books, please answer questions 3-5;
otherwise go directly to question 6.

3) What do you like most about GIRL TALK books?

Check one: Characters_____ Situations_____
                    Telephone Talk_____Other_____

4) Who is your favorite GIRL TALK character?

Check one: Sabrina____ Katie_____ Randy_____
Allison_____ Stacy_____ Other (give name) _____

5) Who is your *least* favorite character?
_____

6) Where did you buy this GIRL TALK book?

Check one: Bookstore____Toy store____Discount store____
Grocery store___Supermarket___Other (give name)_____

Please turn over to continue survey.

7) How many GIRL TALK books have you read?
Check one: 0_____   1 to 2_____   3 to 4 _____   5 or more_____

8) In what type of store would you look for GIRL TALK books?
Bookstore_____Toy store_____Discount store_____
Grocery store_____Supermarket_____Other (give name)_____

9) Which type of store would you visit most often if you
wanted to buy a GIRL TALK book?
Check *only* one: Bookstore_____Toy store_____
Discount store_____Grocery store_____Supermarket_____
Other (give name)_____

10) How many books do you read in a month?
Check one: 0_____   1 to 2_____   3 to 4 _____   5 or more_____

11) Do you read any of these books?
Check those you have read:
The Baby-sitters Club_____   Nancy Drew_____
Pen Pals_____   Sweet Valley High _____
Sweet Valley Twins_____Gymnasts_____

12) Where do you shop most often to buy these books?
Check one: Bookstore_____Toy store_____
Discount store_____Grocery store_____Supermarket_____
Other (give name)_____

13) What other kinds of books do you read most often?
_____

14) What would you like to read more about in GIRL TALK?
_____
_____

Send completed form to :
GIRL TALK Survey, Western Publishing Company, Inc.
1220 Mound Avenue, Mail Station #85
Racine, Wisconsin 53404

LOOK FOR THE AWESOME GIRL TALK BOOKS IN A STORE NEAR YOU!

MORE GIRL TALK TITLES TO LOOK FOR

Nonfiction

ASK ALLIE 101 answers to your questions about boys, friends, family, and school!

YOUR PERSONALITY QUIZ Fun, easy quizzes to help you discover the real you!

BOYTALK: HOW TO TALK TO YOUR FAVORITE GUY